The Chocolate Feast

by
Neil Hollander

illustrations by
Tim Jaques

FREDERICK WARNE

To the guests at my own Chocolate Feast :
Howard, Jesse, Nancy, Maggie,
Osyth, Chantal, Pamela, Anne,
Harald, Charles, Mikki, Nadia
and Irmela

Jonathan Sweet
requests the pleasure of your company
at a Chocolate Feast, to be held on
Chocolate Day, May 26th, at 5 o'clock

MENU

CHOCOLATE SOUP

CHOCOLATE SALAD

CHOCOLATE FONDUE

CHOCOLATE SOUFFLE

CHOCOLATE CAKE

CHOCOLATE SODA

PBET – Please Bring an Empty Tummy

Every year on May 26th Jonathan Sweet celebrates Chocolate Day with a special feast, a Chocolate Feast, where he eats nothing but chocolate from soup to dessert. Chocolate Day, as all chocolate lovers know, is the anniversary of the opening of the first London chocolate shop in 1657.

Of course, Jonathan celebrates other important days with chocolate too, like his birthday, Christmas, the beginning of the football season or the end of school. A Chocolate Feast is the best way to celebrate anything.

No one loves chocolate more than Jonathan. If he has to eat ordinary food, like mashed potatoes or meat, he imagines it is a fluffy chocolate soufflé or a steak-sized bar of milk chocolate.

When he isn't thinking about chocolate he is asleep, and when he is asleep he has chocolate dreams. Sometimes he dreams

he is diving into a chocolate lake filled with ice-cream icebergs.

And sometimes he is trapped in a chocolate prison. The only way to escape is to **eat** his way out.

So he sent one invitation to his dentist, another to the Head Mistress of his school, and the last to his Great Aunt Anne in Saskatchewan.

This year, when Jonathan saw Chocolate Day approaching on the calendar, he planned his menu.

Who would be his guests? All his friends were chocolate lovers and he was sure they would come, every one of them.

They would crowd into the kitchen and devour the chocolate soups and salads and sodas as fast as he could make them. Perhaps it would be wiser to invite people who had never been to a Chocolate Feast before. It might be a surprise for them.

"And if they don't come," Jonathan said to himself, "well, there will be just that much more chocolate for me!"

Early on Chocolate Day morning Jonathan went into his
kitchen and set to work.
The moment he unwrapped the first chocolate bar, his dog
Scraps appeared, barking for his share. Scraps never waited to
be asked to a Chocolate Feast. His nose was his invitation.

Like all good cooks, a chocolate cook must work slowly and
carefully. So, step by step, Jonathan followed the directions in
his Chocolate Cookbook.

Chocolate

100 g (4 oz) chocolate

1 tablespoon flour

Pinch of salt

A bowl

A tablespoon

3 cups milk

3 tablespoons sugar

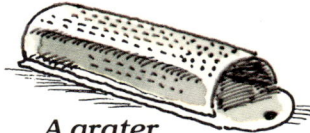
A grater

A wooden spoon

A saucepan

1 Carefully grate the chocolate **2** Put the flour and chocolate in the bowl. Add 4 tablespoons of milk and mix well **3** Pour the rest of the milk into the saucepan. Mix the sugar and salt **4** Heat the saucepan on a low flame until it boils

Soup

5 Add the chocolate-flour mixture and stir well
6 Let the mixture boil gently for 3 minutes

7 Serve the soup hot

Chocolate

2 large chocolate bars

A saucepan

A pan

A sheet of white paper

A sheet of waxed paper

Several lettuce leaves

A bowl

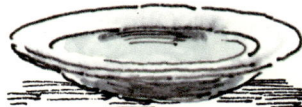

A plate

A greaseproof paper piping bag

1 Break the chocolate into squares, then place them in a saucepan over a low flame, OR, better still, in a bowl suspended in a pan of hot water **2** Let the chocolate melt **3** For carrots and radishes: on a sheet of paper trace the outlines of vegetable leaves in black crayon **4** Cover the paper with a sheet of waxed paper so that the outlines show through

Salad

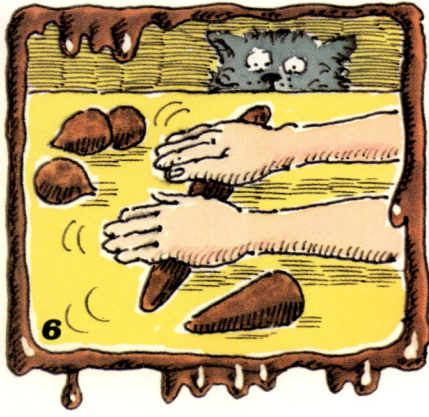

5 Fill a greaseproof piping bag with melted chocolate, and squeeze on to the waxed paper, filling in the outlined shapes. Leave to set **6** Roll lumps of half-melted chocolate into carrot-shaped cones and radish-sized balls

9 Place the chocolate vegetables on top of the chocolate lettuce or cabbage

7 Carefully remove the waxed paper, and join the leaves to the vegetables on a plate **8** For lettuce or cabbage: spread the chocolate evenly on the insides of the leaves with the back of a spoon. Place in the refrigerator to cool, then peel off the lettuce or cabbage leaves and throw them away

Chocolate

150 g (6 oz)
unsweetened
chocolate

Pinch of salt

Banana slices

A saucepan

A fondue pot

1 cup light cream

Pineapple chunks

A tablespoon

A bowl

½ cup butter

Orange sections

Long forks

A candle

1¼ cups sugar

1 teaspoon instant coffee

Whole strawberries

1 Heat the chocolate and cream over a very low flame until the chocolate melts. Mix well   **2** Stir in the sugar, butter and salt

Fondue

3 Put the coffee powder in a bowl and dissolve with
3 tablespoons of water. Then add it to the saucepan
4 Stirring constantly, cook the mixture until it is smooth

5 Pour it into the fondue pot
and place it over the candle

6 Spear pieces of fruit with the
forks and dip into the fondue

Chocolate

75 g (3 oz) butter

4 eggs

A roasting tin

75 g (3 oz) flour

75 g (3 oz) caster sugar

A wooden spoon

30 ml (1 tbs) unsweetened cocoa

A saucepan

A whisk

400 ml (¾ pint) milk

A deep soufflé dish

2 bowls

1 Grease the inside of the soufflé dish with a little butter
2 Break the eggs and separate them – whites in one bowl, yolks in the other   **3** Melt the butter in a saucepan over a low flame   **4** Add the flour and cocoa. Mix well, and cook until the mixture comes away from the sides of the pan

Soufflé

5 Add the milk. Mix well and cook until the sauce is thick   **6** Take the pan off the stove, let it cool for a few minutes, then mix in the egg yolks, one by one
7 Whisk the egg whites until they become lumpy. Then whisk in the sugar until the mixture is stiff

8 Gently mix the egg whites into the sauce

9 Pour the mixture into the soufflé dish, then bake in a hot oven (200°C., 400°F.) for 50 minutes

Chocolate

What you need...

A mixing bowl

A mixing spoon

A wire rack

A teaspoon

A piping bag

What you do...

75 g (3 oz) unsweetened chocolate

½ cup butter

½ teaspoon salt

2¼ cups cake flour

2½ cups demerara sugar

1 cup water

3 eggs

1½ teaspoons vanilla extract

1 cup sour cream

1 carton of double cream

A 30 cm (9 in) cake tin

2 teaspoons baking powder

2 saucepans

An electric mixer

1

2

3

1 Grease and flour the cake tin, then set aside **2** Melt the chocolate in a saucepan over a very low flame, then set aside **3** Put the butter in the mixing bowl and mash it with a spoon until it is smooth **4** Add the sugar and eggs **5** Beat with the electric mixer on high speed for about 5 minutes

4

5

Cake

6 Add the vanilla, melted chocolate, baking powder, and salt, then beat on a low speed
7 Slowly add the flour and sour cream and continue beating until the mixture is smooth
8 Put the water in a saucepan and bring it to a boil. Then pour it into the mixture and blend it with a spoon **9** Pour into the cake tin **10** Bake at 350°F (180°C) for 45 minutes
11 Cool in the tin for 15 minutes, then turn out on to the rack

12 Whip the cream stiffly in the electric mixer and spoon into the piping bag. Decorate the cake with cream

Chocolate

What you need...

What you need...

½ cup cold milk

Whipped cream

2 maraschino cherries

A bowl

¼ cup chocolate syrup

1 bottle chilled soda water

A mixing spoon

4 scoops chocolate ice cream

2 tall glasses

What you do...

1 Mix the milk and chocolate syrup in the bowl   **2** Pour the mixture into the two glasses   **3** Add one scoop of ice cream to each glass   **4** Pour a little soda water into each glass

Soda

5 Mash the ice cream until it is soft   6 Add a second scoop of ice cream to each glass   7 Fill the glasses with soda water   8 Add two full tablespoons of whipped cream

9 Place a cherry on top

At five o'clock the Chocolate Feast was nearly ready. Jonathan
set the table, then mixed the sodas.
But no one came.
He slowly heated the fondue and poured the soup into the bowls.
Still none of the guests arrived.
Jonathan waited a few minutes more, then he said to Scraps,
"What a shame! We'll have to eat it all ourselves."

"Just in time, I see," said Grandbar, as he sat down and tasted the soup with a finger. "Who else is coming?"
"No one, it seems," said Jonathan.
"Good," replied Grandbar. "That's more chocolate for us."
But just as he raised his soda for a toast there was a knock at the door.

At that moment his grandfather, Grandbar, walked in. Everyone called him Grandbar because he always had a big bar of chocolate… or two or three… loose in his pockets. Shaking hands with him was like putting your fingers inside a warm chocolate wrapper.

"I smelt chocolate," said Pam, who lived across the street. "So I came right over."
"All chocolate lovers are welcome," said Jonathan, trying hard to mean it.
"Then my cousins can come too," said Pam. "They're always ready for a chocolate feast."
"Well… perhaps a few," Jonathan muttered, but in rushed a host of cousins who had been listening behind the door. Jonathan and Grandbar set more places at the table.

"What's this?" exclaimed the milkman, peering in at the window. "A Chocolate Day Feast, is it? And no cream. That will never do. But don't worry, I've got plenty of cream, a whole lorry full. I've got sweet cream, whipping cream, clotted cream, single cream, double cream and ice cream. Don't start without me!"

He disappeared, but was back in a minute, his arms loaded with cartons and bottles of cream.

"Shall I make a Chocolate Day speech?" he asked.
"There's no time for speeches," said Jonathan. "The soup is getting cold."
"To Chocolate Day!" proclaimed Pam as she held up her glass.
"And to Jonathan, the chocolate cook! Long live Chocolate!"
"I'm afraid there won't be enough," Grandbar whispered to Jonathan.
"We'll just have to cook some more," he replied.

While Jonathan and Grandbar worked feverishly in the kitchen, everyone clinked their glasses and the feast began.
"Have some more cream," the milkman kept saying.
"Why not?" Pam always replied.
"Another soda?" asked Jonathan from the kitchen.
"Please," said the milkman.
"Make ours doubles," said the cousins.
"Drinks for the house!" cried the milkman, as he handed Grandbar two more bottles of cream.

They all had seconds, then thirds and even fourths. When the pots and platters were empty, they licked the bowls, whisks, teaspoons, tablespoons and mixing spoons until not a drop of chocolate was left in the kitchen.

"Only 364 more days till next Chocolate Day," said Pam wistfully, as she got up to leave.

"Thanks for the Chocolate Feast," said the cousins all together. Then they left as quickly as they had come. The milkman's stomach was as round as a cake. "That was the best Chocolate Feast I've ever had," he said, and he slowly staggered back to his lorry.

Grandbar looked at all the empty dishes.
"I hardly got a taste," he said.
"I didn't even get that," replied Jonathan
sadly. "And there's nothing left for Scraps
either. My first Chocolate Day without
Chocolate!"

Suddenly, the door burst open. There stood his dentist, his Head Mistress, and Great Aunt Anne from Saskatchewan.

The dentist held a chocolate cake shaped like a giant tooth, its cavity filled with frosting. The Head Mistress carried a whole alphabet, A to Z, made of chocolate, and Great Aunt Anne opened a suitcase full of chocolate cookies.

"Happy Chocolate Day!" they shouted.

"Let's begin the Chocolate Feast!"